Rosebud & Red Flannel

by Ethel Pochocki · illustrated by Mary Beth Owens

Down East Books Camden, Maine

A pair of long johns and a nightgown hung side by side on a clothesline, so close that their sleeves almost touched. But they never spoke to each other. Red Flannel, the long johns, said nothing because he was shy and clumsy in the company of someone so beautiful. Rosebud, the nightgown, ignored him because she felt it beneath her dignity to speak with such a coarse fellow.

On some days Rosebud would converse politely with the silk blouses and the lace-edged tablecloth, or now and then with the embroidered guest towels. But while she felt it her duty to be civil with her equals, she did not encourage them to become familiar.

Red Flannel, although he was too shy to talk, would almost tie himself into knots trying to get the nightgown's attention. Every wash day he waved and clapped and flung his legs into the air, dancing with the wind, until he had the socks and the aprons and the underpants laughing so hard they wound themselves around the line.

This merry company (except for Rosebud) enjoyed their weekly
roughhousing in the sun. Sometimes, in a stiff, brisk wind, the sheets
blew up like hot-air balloons and the line of bath towels, marching
like soldiers, smacked each other in sharp good humor. And all the
while Red Flannel somersaulted about, trying to impress his love.

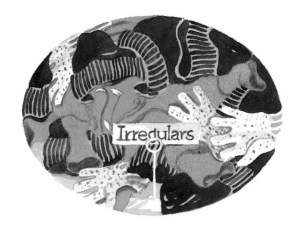

Red Flannel was older than Rosebud, but he felt as chipper as when he'd first appeared under the Christmas tree two years ago. The mistress had found him on a table of marked-down bargains at the Army-Navy surplus store. IRREGULARS the sign had read. He had been dumped there out of a box sent from the woolen mill, one bright-red splash amid the unraveling caps and gloves.

The mistress ignored his imperfections (a thread snipped here, a button tightened there, all would be well) and snapped him up as a gift for her husband.

Red Flannel's wool was thinner now, a bit scratchy from many washings, and he had a plaid patch on one knee, but neither his spirit nor his color had faded in the winter sun.

Rosebud had come to the house just this past Christmas, and she was not happy with her lot. "I was made for a gentle life, a lady's life," she sighed, "not for hobnobbing with peasants. Oh, I suppose dish towels and aprons have their place. It's just that we have nothing in common. What do *I* have to do with their silly kitchen gossip?"

She remembered the exquisite care that had gone into fashioning her—how the old ladies with their knobby fingers had sewn lace around her neck. She remembered their musical French chatter as they'd spread her out on the coverlet, marveling over what they had made. To think she had traveled over an ocean to end up shivering on a clothesline next to this clowning oaf who couldn't speak a sensible sentence!

But as the wash days passed, Rosebud realized that she couldn't improve things by sulking.

"A thing of beauty soon withers in the damp of self-pity," she told herself, admiring such a deep thought. She resolved to find some small thing to enjoy each day. Today she rejoiced in the bright-blue sky, and thought how lovely she must look against it. She dangled gracefully from the wooden clothespins, and Red Flannel's heart flipped as she accidentally brushed against him.

He flapped his arms and threw his legs over the line. As usual she ignored him. She could tell by the cast of the sun that it was almost mid-afternoon—time for the mistress to come and gather the clothes into a large wicker basket. She would fluff up the nightgown and hold her to her face, sighing, "Oh, you are so beautiful, I shall keep you forever!"

But on this day the mistress didn't come, for she had gone to the village for groceries. The bright-blue sky began to darken, turning sullen and very quiet, as if it knew something was going to happen.

Slowly snow began to fall, little dancing flakes at first, then larger, heavier ones. They turned to hard crystal pellets that made a pittering sound as they hit the ground and trees. Houses and roads disappeared, and soon only the snowplow's headlights could pierce the white curtain.

Rosebud was terrified. Never had she been in a snowstorm!

Red Flannel, though, had survived several such squalls, and had even been frozen once. He shuddered at the memory: He had been dancing in the wind, but when the snows had come, he could neither bend nor move. He'd heard his legs creak against the clothesline as if they were boards. For a whole day he'd hung, frozen as a statue. Finally, when the storm died, the mistress had brought him into the kitchen to thaw.

Now he feared that this might happen again. And what of his love, so sweet, so fragile? How could he protect her? Already the bath towels and the hunting socks had stiffened. He could not feel his legs. He must act quickly, before the ice took his arms.

For the first time, Red Flannel spoke to the nightgown.

"Sweet Rosebud, listen to me—can you move?"

One of her clothespins had been whipped off by the wind, and she dangled by one shoulder. "Yes, I . . . I think so. But I feel heavy, and the lace at my wrist is hard. . . ." She was so frightened, she spoke to the long johns as if he were her equal.

"Quickly, then," Red Flannel said. "When the next gust of wind comes, lean toward me. Quickly, before my arms freeze. Here comes a good one. Now, *jump!*" At that moment the wind tore off Rosebud's other clothespin, and the nightgown fell into the arms of the long johns. Red Flannel wrapped them around her tightly so that, when they froze, she would be safe within them. He couldn't think beyond that.

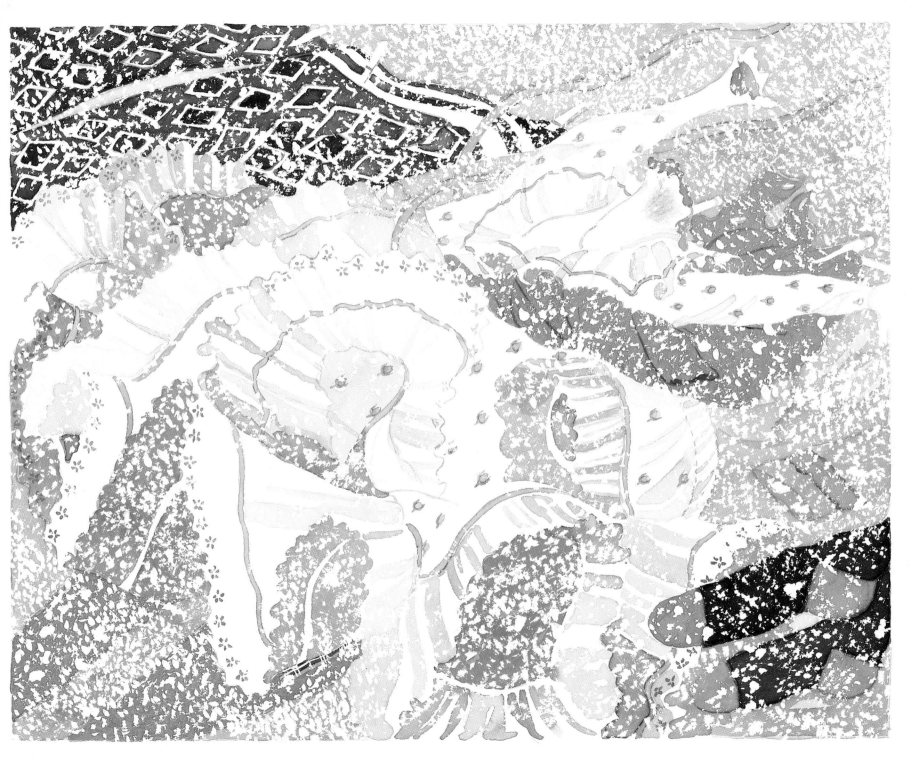

The wind gathered its strength for one final, terrible blast. It tore the towels and the tablecloths and the long johns off the line and sent them whirling up, up into the sky and out of sight.

By the time the wind wearied and the snowflakes turned gentle again, the mistress had returned. She and her children and her husband searched and searched for the missing wash, but only the red-gingham tablecloth was ever found, atop a neighbor's doghouse. The mistress grieved for her lovely nightgown. She had owned it only a month.

Rosebud and Red Flannel had landed in a farmer's meadow several towns away. There they lay, frozen together under the snow.
When spring came and the snow melted, they thawed in the sun.

When they awoke, Rosebud found that her heart had also thawed. She knew now that this fellow she'd once thought common was a true gentleman, of such courage that he would give his life for her.

And because he knew his love was returned, Red Flannel no longer felt shy and clumsy.

When the frozen earth turned to spring mud, they heard
the cows plodding up to the haystack where they lay. The farm
animals chewed at Rosebud's ribbon and nuzzled Red
Flannel's legs.

"Oh, dear," he worried. "Now what? Have we lived this long
just to be eaten by cows? Do they think we are hay?"

Rosebud felt muddy hooves walking over her, and she sobbed,
remembering the ladies sewing her delicate collar.

"Here, what's this?" asked a gruff voice. A farmer stood above them, hands on hips, eyebrows bristling. "How in tarnation did a pair of red flannels and a nightie get into my pasture?" He laughed, and picked them up and brought them to his wife.

"I know just what to do with them," she said with a smile.

So the farmer's wife stuffed them with straw and gave them backbones of wood, and Red Flannel guarded the cornfield while Rosebud fluttered over the cabbages.

And all summer long they called out to each other.

"Red Flannel, my love, tell me a joke!"

"Rosebud, my darling, sing me a song!"

All day they joked and sang and told their deepest thoughts to each other, and at night they danced in the moonlight to the music of the crickets.

For Virginia Gray, with love   —E.P.

For Betty Gilmore —M.B.O.

Text copyright © 1989 by Ethel Pochocki
Ilustrations copyright © 1991 by Mary Beth Owens
All rights reserved, including the right to reproduce this book or portions thereof in any form.
Reprinted 1999 by arrangement with the author and illustrator.
Originally published by Henry Holt and Company, Inc., in 1991.

ISBN 0-89272-474-9

Printed by Oceanic Graphic Printing, Inc., Hong Kong

10   9   8   7   6   5   4   3   2   1

Down East Books
P.O. Box 679
Camden, ME 04843
Book Orders: 1-800-685-7962

Library of Congress Cataloging-in-Publication Data

Pochocki, Ethel, 1925–
        Rosebud and Red Flannel / Ethel Pochocki ; illustrations by Mary Beth Owens.
                p.   cm.
        "A different version of the text . . . was published in *Cricket* magazine
under the title Red Flannel and Rosebud in 1989"—T.p. verso.
        Summary: A snobbish nightgown finds true love with a shy pair of
long johns after they are blown off their clothesline in a snowstorm.
        ISBN 0-89272-474-9
        [1. Underwear Fiction. 2. Nightgowns Fiction.] I. Owens, Mary Beth, ill. II. Title.
[PZ7.P7495Ro 1999]
[E]—dc21   99-35563
                                                                              CIP